The First Starry Night

Whispering Coyote
A Charlesbridge Imprint

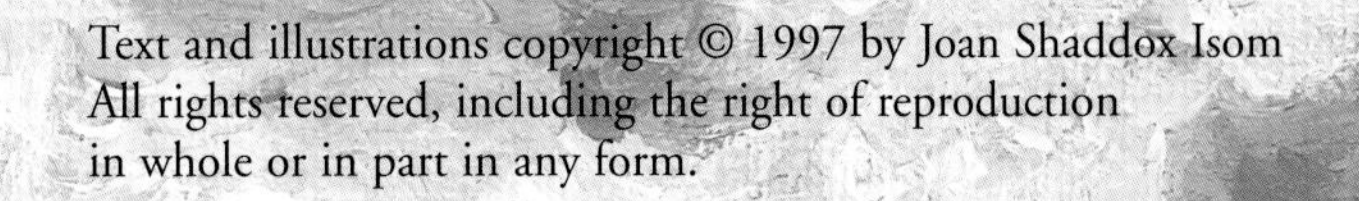

A Whispering Coyote Book
Published by Charlesbridge Publishing
85 Main Street
Watertown, MA 02472
(617) 926-0329
www.charlesbridge.com

Library of Congress Cataloging–in–Publication Data

Isom, Joan Shaddox.
The first starry night / written and illustrated by Joan S. Isom.
p. cm.
Summary: Jacques encounters and befriends Vincent van Gogh when he comes to stay in the boarding house where he works.
ISBN 1-879085-96-8 (reinforced for library use)
ISBN 1-58089-027-X (softcover)
1. Gogh, Vincent van, 1853-1890—Juvenile fiction. [1. Gogh, Vincent van, 1853-1890—Fiction. 2. Artists—Fiction. 3. France—Fiction.] I. Title.
PZ7.I8385F1 1998
[Fic]—dc21 97-33372

Printed in China
(hc)10 9 8 7 6 5 4 3
(sc)10 9 8 7 6 5 4 3 2 1

Display type and text type set in Bergell and 15-point Garamond.
Separated and manufactured by Toppan Printing Company
Book production and design by *The Kids at Our House*

To everyone who has found
a brother or a sister of the heart,
and for those who are still searching

My name is Jacques. I wash pots and pans in Madame Rouel's kitchen. She pays me with bread and cheese. I get an extra piece of bread if I do a good job. An artist lives and works upstairs. He has a red beard. I want to see what he paints, so I sneak up the stairs and peek in when he is not looking. Madame Rouel's cat goes with me.

The man's name is Vincent. Some people are afraid of him. But I see him buying bread to feed the dogs in the street. I see him petting the cat. I think he is a kind man.

Vincent paints pictures with suns like golden pumpkins. He paints pictures of people at work in the fields. I like his art so much that I forget to hide. Vincent sees me.

"Hello," he says in a gruff voice. "Please sit down. You may watch me paint if you will not make a pest of yourself. Why aren't you afraid of me? The other children are."

"Because I see you feeding the stray dogs. And Melon the cat likes you."

"And what if I talk to myself?" he asks.

"I do that too, when I'm working in the kitchen alone. But now we can talk to each other," I tell him. "My name is Jacques."

"And I am Vincent." He smears a blob of paint onto his canvas. As I watch, it turns into a corn shock.

Melon and I visit our friend every day. Melon likes to sit under Vincent's window and watch crows eat the sunflower seeds. I think Vincent likes the cat because she is his favorite color.

My friend and I talk. I share my extra bread with him. He tells me, "I walk in the fields and make drawings. Then, I bring them home and sometimes I make them into paintings."

"Madame Rouel told me to run if you start to throw paint or brushes," I say. "I told her not to worry. I can run very fast."

Vincent laughs for a long time. He no longer looks fierce. "Someday you will sell a painting and you can buy a whole wheel of cheese as fat as a cat, as yellow as the sun!" I tell him.

"Look here, Jacques," Vincent says, "you worry too much about food. Tomorrow you must finish your work early and go with me. I will show you a place where corn shocks are a dozen different tints of gold, and their shadows are shades of violet."

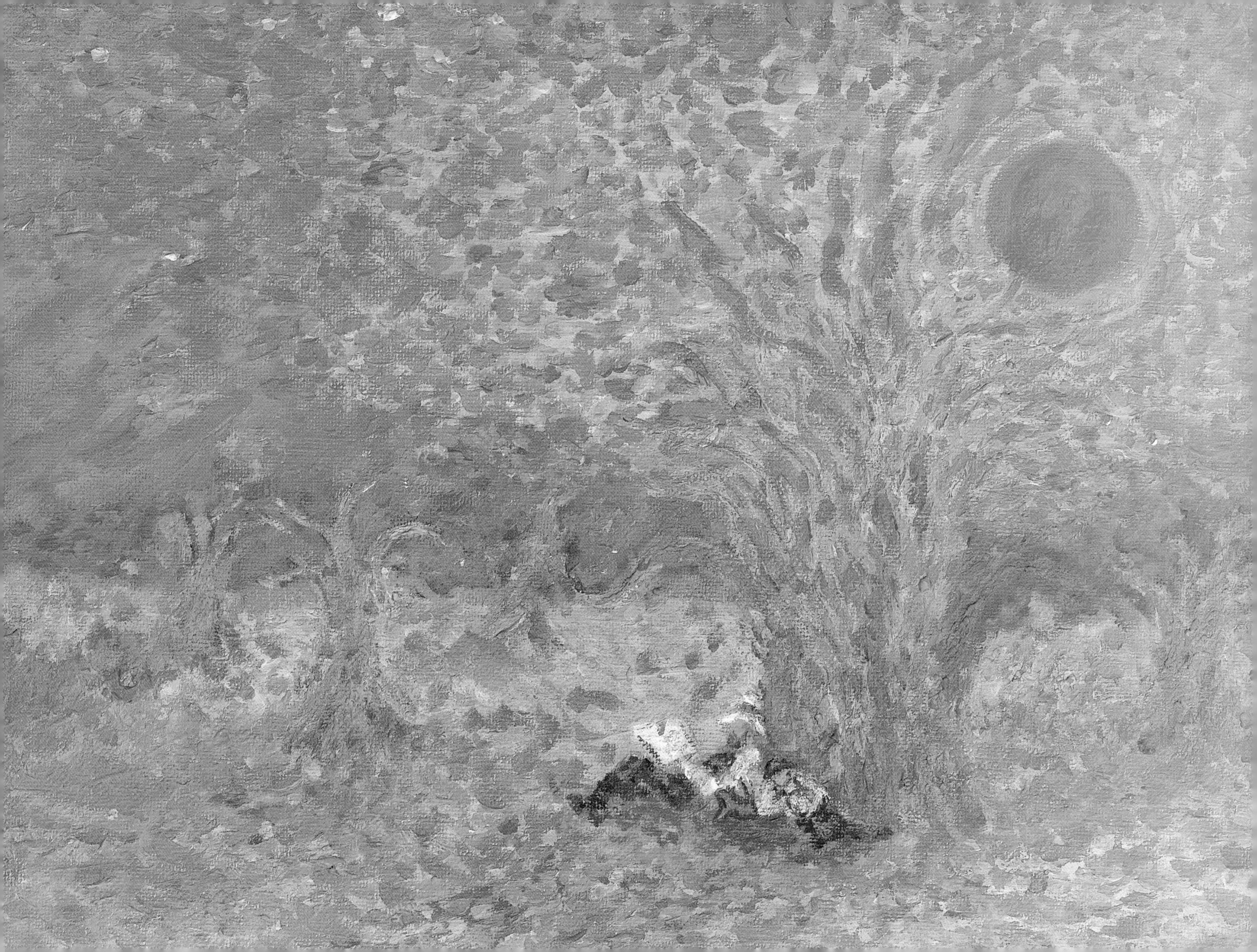

My friend loves to take long walks. He says he dreamed of the smell of the plowed fields when he was in Paris. He says he loves to feel the warm, sweet wind on his skin. He paints pictures of the trees and the meadows when they blossom in the springtime. In autumn, he paints pictures of the grain as it turns golden. "Look, Jacques," he says. "See how the sky is the color of a cornflower at noon, and how it changes to the color of Melon in the evening."

Once it snowed, and he painted a picture of the lights as they spilled from the shop windows.

Vincent says he can paint at night if I hold candles for him. I try to help, but I fall asleep. When I wake up, I see he has stuck candles in his hatband and is bending over his canvas. When I look at this painting of the stars, I know it will be my favorite.

"Why do you love the stars so much?" I ask Vincent.

"Maybe because they are like a good painting or a good story. They stay," he tells me.

"But the stars don't really look the way you have painted them," I tell him.

Vincent studies my face as he puffs at his pipe. Finally, he asks, "How do you know how *I* see the stars, Jacques?"

"And why do you keep making pictures and more pictures, when you never sell a one?" I ask Vincent.

"And why do you ask so many questions?" Vincent says, as he starts another picture.

I go to the kitchen. Madame Rouel gives me half a loaf of bread! She pours milk and hot coffee into a blue pot and tells me I can have it with my bread. She says I did an especially good job cleaning her big black stove. I run to my friend's studio.

"Look, Vincent! Half a loaf, and *cafe au lait*, all for us!" I tell him.

Vincent is happy. "See here, Jacques. Let's use the blue tablecloth and the yellow vase of flowers." He spreads the cloth on his little table and sets it with orange plates and blue cups.

He breaks the bread in two and hands me the bigger piece. He dunks his bread into his coffee and begins to eat. "Ah, Jacques," he says, "Is there anything better than fresh bread and hot coffee, shared with a good, good friend?"

As we eat, I pretend he is my older brother, but I don't tell anyone, not even Melon.

Vincent asks, "Where do you live, Jacques?"

"I live here," I say. "I sleep on a cot in a corner of the kitchen. I wash at the pump outside."

He asks about my parents and I tell him I have none.

My friend is quiet for a long time. Finally he speaks. "You and I, Jacques, are much alike. I too have no home of my own."

"You say you have a brother," I tell him. "I wish I had a brother."

"But Jacques, there are many kinds of brothers. I have a good brother, Theo. Without him, I could not live. But you and I, Jacques, are brothers of the heart."

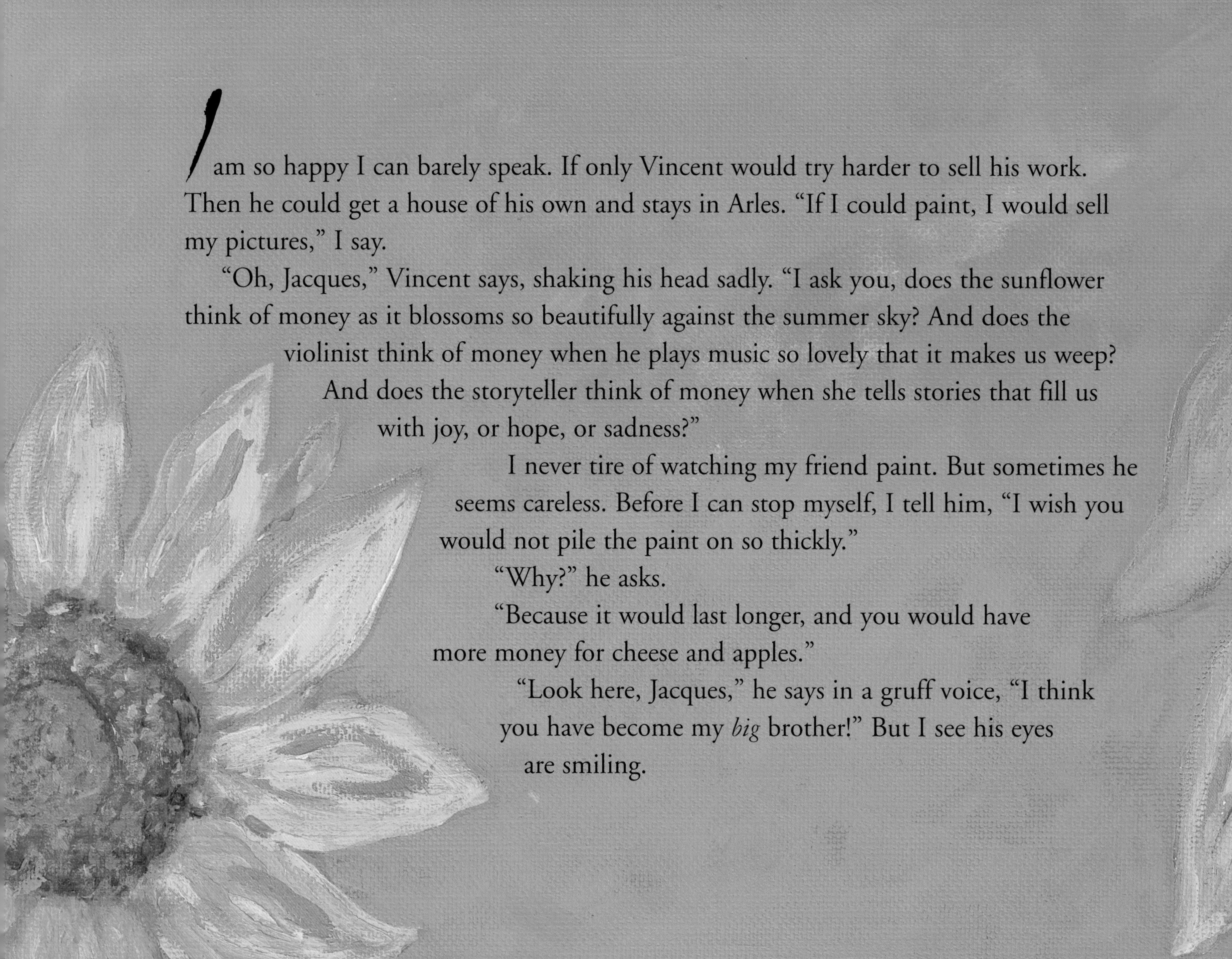

I am so happy I can barely speak. If only Vincent would try harder to sell his work. Then he could get a house of his own and stays in Arles. "If I could paint, I would sell my pictures," I say.

"Oh, Jacques," Vincent says, shaking his head sadly. "I ask you, does the sunflower think of money as it blossoms so beautifully against the summer sky? And does the violinist think of money when he plays music so lovely that it makes us weep? And does the storyteller think of money when she tells stories that fill us with joy, or hope, or sadness?"

I never tire of watching my friend paint. But sometimes he seems careless. Before I can stop myself, I tell him, "I wish you would not pile the paint on so thickly."

"Why?" he asks.

"Because it would last longer, and you would have more money for cheese and apples."

"Look here, Jacques," he says in a gruff voice, "I think you have become my *big* brother!" But I see his eyes are smiling.

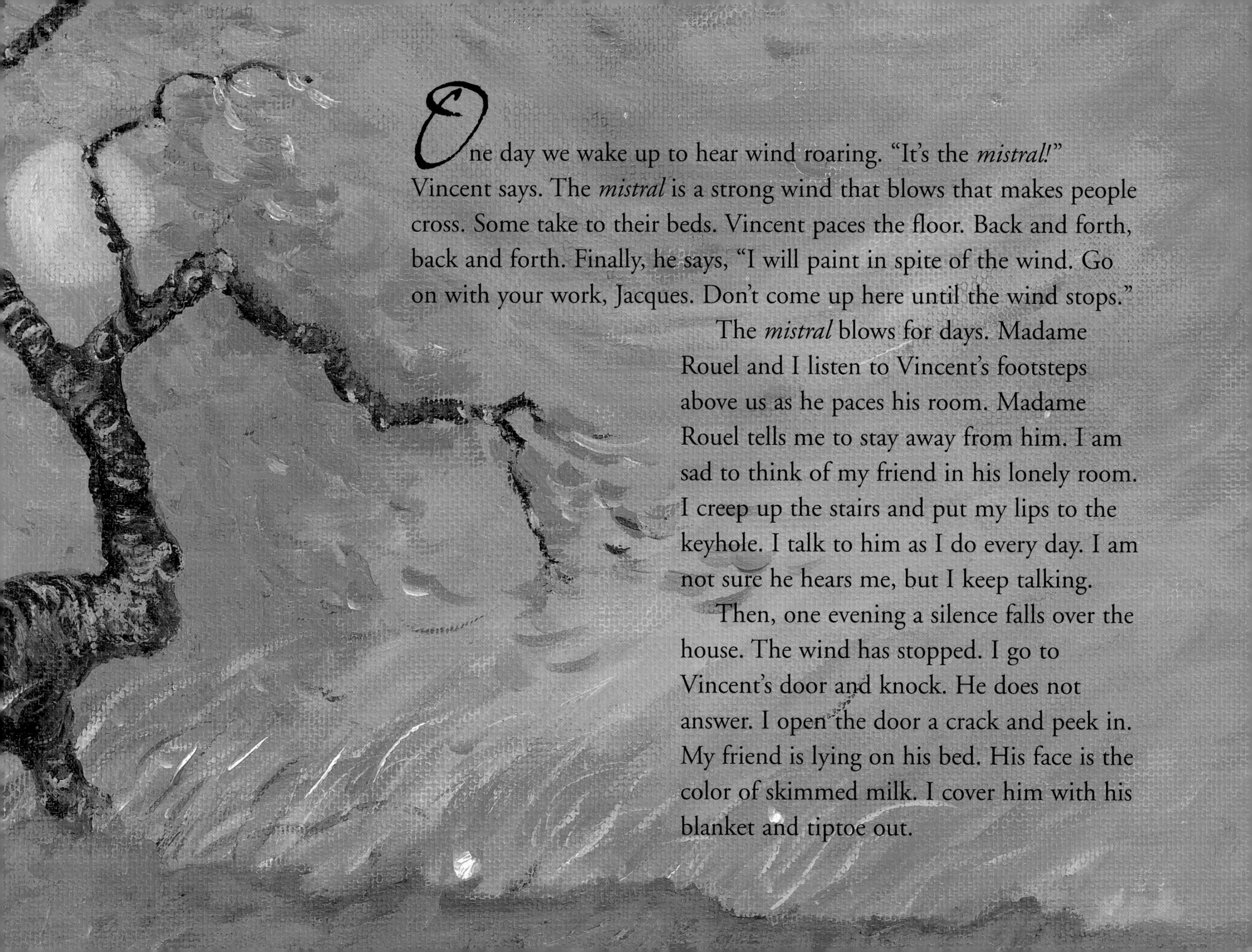

One day we wake up to hear wind roaring. "It's the *mistral!*" Vincent says. The *mistral* is a strong wind that blows that makes people cross. Some take to their beds. Vincent paces the floor. Back and forth, back and forth. Finally, he says, "I will paint in spite of the wind. Go on with your work, Jacques. Don't come up here until the wind stops."

The *mistral* blows for days. Madame Rouel and I listen to Vincent's footsteps above us as he paces his room. Madame Rouel tells me to stay away from him. I am sad to think of my friend in his lonely room. I creep up the stairs and put my lips to the keyhole. I talk to him as I do every day. I am not sure he hears me, but I keep talking.

Then, one evening a silence falls over the house. The wind has stopped. I go to Vincent's door and knock. He does not answer. I open the door a crack and peek in. My friend is lying on his bed. His face is the color of skimmed milk. I cover him with his blanket and tiptoe out.

The next day, Vincent seems rested. "Jacques," he says, "your voice helped me to block out the terrible wind. My studio is full of paintings. I must send some to my brother. Perhaps he can sell some of them."

"And you will have lots of money! Not that you want a lot of money," I added quickly.

In a few weeks a letter comes. Vincent opens it and finds money from his brother. "A painting has sold, Jacques!" he says.

Vincent buys a huge wheel of cheese, some crimson apples, a whole loaf of crusty bread, and some orange and blue flowers. And for Melon, he has a fish.

Now I think Vincent will sell many paintings. But that does not happen.

One day I go to his studio. The room is dark. Vincent has packed all his paintings into a big trunk. He is packing his clothes into a little bag. “Why are you leaving?” I ask.

“Remember, I told you when we first met that I would leave someday?”

“But we have not done all the things we planned!” I say.

“I am sorry, Jacques. But I will write to you,” he says. He opens the trunk that holds his paintings. Light floods the room. He takes some of the paintings from the trunk. One is of the sky with pinwheel stars. It is the one he painted the night I awoke to find his hat glowing with candles like a strange birthday cake.

He stacks five of the paintings in the corner and covers them with a cloth. "Now, I must pack the rest of my things and go. And Jacques, I have arranged for you to attend school here in Arles. Madame Rouel will see that you have what you need. You must learn quickly so that you can read my letters and write to me."

Vincent closes the lid on the trunk that holds the rest of his paintings. The light leaves the room once more.

I will not come to this place again.

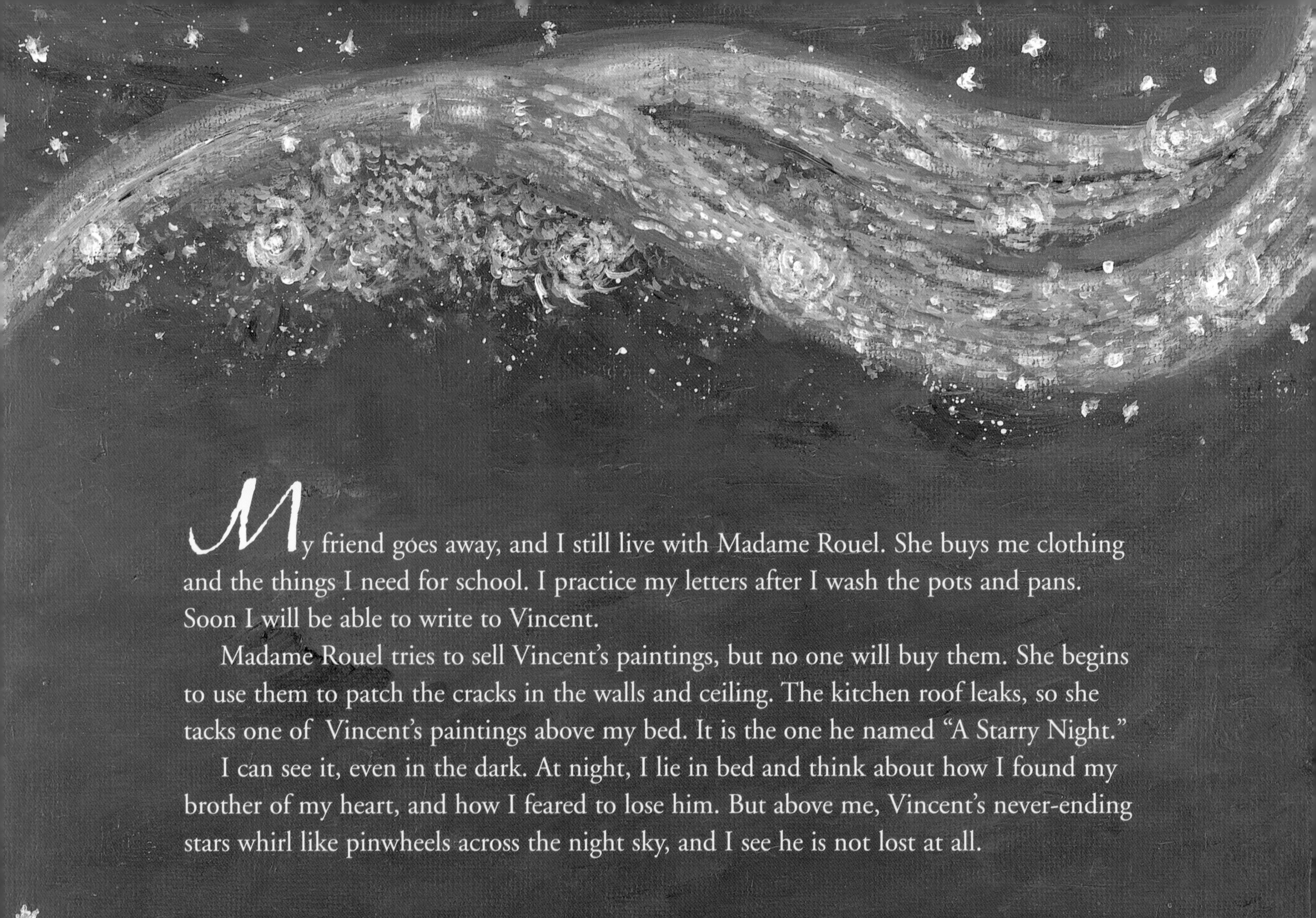

My friend goes away, and I still live with Madame Rouel. She buys me clothing and the things I need for school. I practice my letters after I wash the pots and pans. Soon I will be able to write to Vincent.

Madame Rouel tries to sell Vincent's paintings, but no one will buy them. She begins to use them to patch the cracks in the walls and ceiling. The kitchen roof leaks, so she tacks one of Vincent's paintings above my bed. It is the one he named "A Starry Night."

I can see it, even in the dark. At night, I lie in bed and think about how I found my brother of my heart, and how I feared to lose him. But above me, Vincent's never-ending stars whirl like pinwheels across the night sky, and I see he is not lost at all.

van GOGH, Vincent.
The Starry Night. (1889)
Oil on Canvas, 29 x 36 1/4" (73.7 x 92.1cm).
The Museum of Modern Art, New York. Acquired through the Lillie P. Bliss Bequest.

Vincent van Gogh(1853–1890), was a Dutch painter who lived and worked for a short time in Arles, France. He painted hundreds of paintings, including three versions of "A Starry Night," but sold only one painting during his lifetime. Many of his paintings were lost; some were used by farmers and peasants to patch the roofs and walls of their homes.